The Stars in My Geddoh's Sky

WRITTEN BY *Claire Sidhom Matze*

ILLUSTRATED BY *Bill Farnsworth*

Albert Whitman & Company
Morton Grove, Illinois

One summer day a roaring bird comes screeching across the sky, carrying my grandfather.

He's here!

Mom and Dad rush to greet him. Everyone talks at once. My heart plays ping-pong in my chest. Should I hug him? Will he know me? I wait, I smile.

He looks at me and opens his arms.

I fly!

"*Habibi*...my dear," he whispers. "Geddoh is here!"

Geddoh? Yes! That's Arabic for grandfather.

When we get home, Dad helps carry the trunks upstairs. "What's in this one, Geddoh?" I ask.

Geddoh hands me a key. "Would you like to open it, Alex?"

I lift up the lid. Clothes, jars, and shiny plates are crammed inside. And underneath, I see this huge brown wood and leather thing. It's not a toy. It's not a chair. And it's so heavy I can't lift it!

"Geddoh, what *is* this?"

"It's a camel saddle for you, Alex. See? You can sit on it, like this, and pretend you're riding across the desert."

Geddoh looks funny on his saddle. When it's my turn, I close my eyes and pretend I'm in a desert storm. The wind is whipping sand around me. I'm miles away from home, but I'm not scared: I know that my camel can go many days without food or water.

I open my eyes. "Thank you for my present, Geddoh. I love it!"

I help Geddoh unpack. He's brought presents for everyone. There are Arabic storybooks and toy camels for me, a chess game for Dad, beautiful jewelry for Mom, a toy snake that is a symbol for long life, and a shiny brass gong with drawings on it.

When we finish unpacking, Geddoh yawns. "I think I'll go to bed now. It's still early here, but in my part of the world it's the middle of the night. I bet I'll be the first one up tomorrow!"

Geddoh's wrong. I beat him to it. When I open my eyes the next day, it's still night. I toss and turn and wait and wait. Just when I feel I can't bear it anymore, I hear him moving in his room. I feel my way to his door and knock once, twice. "Shhhh!" Geddoh whispers. "You'll wake up the town!"

After breakfast, Geddoh says, "At home I usually eat a big meal at noon. Do you want to help me fix lunch? We'll surprise the family."

As the sun comes up, we pick leaves from the grapevine in my yard. He shows me how to stuff them with rice and the special spices he's brought.

We make *konafa* for dessert. I pick rose petals to flavor the water for the syrup. We coat some shredded wheat and nuts in butter. He lets me pack the mixture in the baking pan while he prepares the thick syrup with rose water. Then he makes coffee so strong it looks like another syrup: this one black!

I bang our new gong when it's time for lunch.

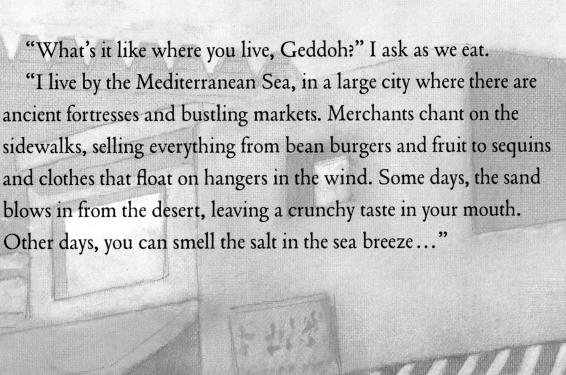

"What's it like where you live, Geddoh?" I ask as we eat.

"I live by the Mediterranean Sea, in a large city where there are ancient fortresses and bustling markets. Merchants chant on the sidewalks, selling everything from bean burgers and fruit to sequins and clothes that float on hangers in the wind. Some days, the sand blows in from the desert, leaving a crunchy taste in your mouth. Other days, you can smell the salt in the sea breeze…"

"Tell me more!"

"My child, how can I paint my country with words? My homeland lies in the most beautiful valley in the world, where palm trees grow heavy with plump red dates.

"In the countryside, farmers till the soil, women gossip over laundry, children swim in the river. Nearby, flat bread bakes in stone ovens and pigeons roast in giant pits.

"From the mosque, five times a day, comes the call to prayer. Then everything stops. Everything but the flow of the river…"

"And for you also, Geddoh? Does everything stop for you?"

Geddoh nods. "Yes, Alex. Before sunrise and at noon, at mid-afternoon and after sunset, and then again in the dark of the night, I pray."

The days go by.

We play catch in the park. I try to teach him baseball. He doesn't know where to run!

We spend time by the ocean, laugh in the wind, and fly a kite on the beach.

I write my name in English on the sand. Then I write Geddoh's. Geddoh writes both our names in Arabic. His writing looks squiggly! I like to see our two names in the sand, in our two languages, side by side.

One evening Mom and Dad go out, and Geddoh says, "Let's take a picnic and go back to the ocean."

We arrive in time to watch the sun dip into the water, splashing the sky with party colors just for us. Geddoh rolls out his prayer mat. I watch him face the east and bow and bend and touch the ground, praying softly in Arabic. Then we share our dinner on the beach.

The days turn into weeks.

I love the gifts Geddoh's given me, but he didn't wrap my favorite one: time, my time with him.

One morning my Geddoh says he has to leave. I throw a rock very hard.

"What's this? Tears?" Gently, Geddoh hugs me.

"No!" I shout. "I don't want you to go! Why can't you just stay forever?"

Geddoh holds me close. "My child, I love you so!
I'd like to stay and watch you grow and share many years
with you. But my homeland is calling me. I miss it!
And when I die, I want to be buried in my land, by
your grandmother."

Quickly he turns away. But not before I've seen the
tears in his eyes.

"Geddoh, will you ever come back? Will I see you
again?"

"Of course, Alex! Soon we'll be making plans for
our next meeting. Who knows, maybe you'll come to
see me next time! Meanwhile, we can write to each other.
Our letters will be a thread of love across the ocean.
Will you do this for me?"

My Dearest Alex,
I miss you
sunset was
remember
your p
comi
in

On our last night together, we take a walk to the cliffs.
Everything is quiet and still, the stars so close I can almost
touch them.

Geddoh points to a constellation that looks like something
flying. "This group of stars is called *Aquila*, which means 'eagle.'
And the brightest star you see over there, my people named *Altair*,
or 'the flying one.' Remember, my child, even when we're apart,
we'll share this sparkling canopy.

"Your sky, your moon, your stars are mine, too, *habibi*, my dear.
And as you look up at Altair, my thoughts will fly to you."

To Granny Andree and Geddoh Samir: I think of you always with love.
To Mark, Gerard, Bernie, Laura, and Sabrina: here is my dream, come true for you.
To Kathy, my editor and friend: many, many thanks!
—C. M.

To my wife, Deborah, and my daughters, Allison and Caitlin.
—B. F.

The constellation Aquila, with its brightest star, Altair.
Geddoh is pronounced GEH⁄doh or JEH⁄doh.

Library of Congress Cataloging⁄in⁄Publication Data

Matze, Claire Sidhom.
The stars in my Geddoh's sky / by Claire Sidhom Matze; illustrated by Bill Farnsworth.
p. cm.
Summary: Alex's Arabic⁄speaking grandfather comes to visit the United States
and Alex learns about his grandfather's Middle Eastern homeland.
ISBN 0⁄8075⁄5332⁄8
[1. Grandfathers—Fiction. 2. Egypt—Fiction.] I. Farnsworth, Bill, ill. II. Title.
PZ7.M43675ST 1999 [E]—DC21 98⁄39185 CIP AC

The illustration medium is oil on linen.
The text is set in Poliphilus.
The design is by Scott Piehl.